To Doris,

a fellow cat Lover; the moral
of this tale is
"Don't believe everything you're
told!"

Yette Funkel
2009

Trudy and the Captain's Cat

YETTI FRENKEL

Snow Tree Books

Trudy sat by the window in the sunshine, gazing out at the city on the first day of spring. Children laughed in the park and sparrows darted past, gathering twigs for their nests.

"Winter has come and gone," she thought, "but nothing exciting has happened. A cat needs some adventure now and then, just for a change of pace."

Mrs. Gardini hurried in, carrying her wicker basket.

"I'm off to the market," she told Trudy. "When I come home, I'll have a nice surprise for you."

Trudy pricked up her ears.

"I'll bet the market is exciting," she thought. "I'll go too."

As soon as Mrs. Gardini left, Trudy squeezed under the window. She was very fat and for a moment she got stuck. She clawed and struggled until she was free, then she hopped onto the fire escape. Mrs. Gardini walked briskly down the street and Trudy followed, careful to keep out of sight.

Soon they came to a crowded square full of brightly painted carts and boxes of vegetables. Trudy slipped beneath a cart and peered out at the busy market. She had never seen so many people, or smelled so much food! Her eyes grew wide when she saw a man in an apron placing fish on a cart of ice.

"Mackerel for sale," he called. "Fresh from the sea."

Trudy's nose tingled with the smell of the fish and her stomach began to rumble.

"I'll just take a look," she thought, stepping closer to the cart.

She reared up on her hind legs and stood face to face with
a mackerel. "No one will notice if I just take one," she thought.
She chose the largest fish in the pile and sat down to eat it,
purring contentedly.

Schwack! A dishtowel struck her back.

"Thieving, good-for-nothing, flea-bitten cat!" snapped the man
in the apron.

"I'll teach you to steal my fish!"

Trudy grabbed the fish and ran. She felt the dishtowel snapping at her heels as she raced through the market, dodging shoppers and leaping over boxes of fruit. The chase went on until they came to a hill. At the bottom of the hill was the sea. A long pier stretched out into the water.

"If he keeps chasing me, I'll have to swim for it," thought Trudy, "and I don't know how to swim!"

But the man in the apron was out of breath. He turned back and trudged up the hill, wiping his brow.

Trudy stopped at the pier. She put the fish down and rested.

"Psst!" said a voice.

Trudy looked around. She saw only a battered old fishing boat tied up at the pier.

"Ahoy mate," said the voice again. "If you've got a fish to share, bring it aboard."

Trudy looked up and saw a large, white cat standing on the deck of the fishing boat.

She picked up the fish and walked along the pier until she found a place to climb on board.

Trudy wobbled as she stepped onto the rocking boat.

"Steady Lass," laughed the cat. "You'll soon get your sea legs. My name's Albi, by the way. Short for Albatross. And your name would be?"

"Trudy," she said. She looked closely at the cat. His fur was long and scruffy and he moved stiffly, like an old cat.

"Have you been a sea cat long?" she asked.

"Aye," said Albi. "Longer than you've been a city cat, to be sure." He looked hungrily at the fish.

"Won't you join me for lunch?" Trudy asked politely.

"Delighted," said Albi. "But why don't we wait a bit? First let me show you around this old tub."

Trudy followed Albi across the rotting planks of the deck.

She sniffed carefully at the piles of rope and tattered nets.

They smelled of salt and seaweed.

"It must be exciting to be on the water," she said, "to see faraway places and ride the waves."

"That it is," agreed Albi. "Many's the time I went fishing with the captain and his son. Sometimes the fog was so thick that I couldn't see my paws. When we pulled in the nets they were full of fish, more fish than you could eat in a year."

Trudy tried to imagine that many fish.

"Once, Mrs. Gardini gave me a can of sardines," she said. "That was the most fish I've ever seen."

"What a landlubber you are," laughed Albi. "You haven't seen much of the world, have you?"

Trudy thought of the comfortable, cheery apartment she shared with Mrs. Gardini.

"No, " she said truthfully, "but I see many things from my window."

Albi's eyes twinkled. "From a window! Trudy, life is to be lived, not seen from a distance."

Trudy closed her eyes. The boat rocked gently beneath her and the salty breeze tickled her nose. She imagined all the things she might have seen if she had been born a sea cat and not a pampered house cat.

"What a wonderful life," she sighed.

Albi nodded thoughtfully. "It was indeed," he said, "but the sea can be a treacherous place. One night a terrible storm blew in. The captain's son was washed overboard. He clung to the railing with one hand and the captain grabbed the other. I saw them both at the rail as the boat rose on a swell. Then a great wave crashed down and they were swallowed by the sea."

Trudy shivered. She remembered how safe and warm Mrs. Gardini's lap felt when a storm raged outside.

"What did you do?" she asked.

"I crouched low on the deck," said Albi. "I knew that I had to ride out the storm alone. The boat rocked wildly and it was all I could do to keep from rolling overboard. Then up went the boat atop a mighty swell. My feet slipped on the deck and I rolled tail over ears into the hold."

"What's a hold?" asked Trudy.

Albi pointed to an opening in the deck. Trudy peered down into a deep, dark hole filled with water. She backed away quickly.

"I wouldn't like to fall down there," she said.

"Aye, it's a scary place for a cat," said Albi. "It's the place where the fish are stored. They wriggled about me as I thrashed in the water, gasping for air. Then the icy water closed over my ears and all went dark."

"That's horrible!" cried Trudy. "How did you manage to get out alive ?"

"I didn't," said Albi with a hollow laugh. "I drowned. What you see, Lass, is the ghost of the captain's cat."

Trudy stared at Albi with large green eyes. The longer she stared at him the more transparent he became, until she could see right through him to the boats sailing in the distance. In one quick leap she reached the top of the railing and jumped down to the pier.

She heard Albi laughing.

"Thanks for the fish, Lass!" he called.

Frightened as she was, Trudy turned to look at him.

He stood on the deck waving to her.

"I've enjoyed your visit," he called. "Come back again, Trudy."

Trudy shuddered and raced along the pier. She ran through streets full of honking, belching cars. Tires screeched and angry drivers shook their fists.

At last she stopped to rest, panting for breath.

There were so many legs, so many shoes on hurrying feet.

"Trudy, what are you doing here?"

Trudy looked up to see Mrs. Gardini standing over her. She scooped Trudy into her arms.

"Naughty cat!" she said. "I thought you were too plump to fit under that window. Well, I'll keep it shut from now on."

Trudy purred as she leaned against Mrs. Gardini. She felt safe and warm and the sea seemed very far away.

Mrs. Gardini put Trudy into her basket.

"I have a treat for you in here," she said. "Let's go home and have lunch."

From deep in the basket Trudy heard her say, "I've never seen you run so fast. I thought you'd seen a ghost."

Trudy purred. She thought of her soft pillow by the window and how good it would feel to be home.

"If you only knew," she thought.

With a sigh of contentment she curled up on the mackerel and went to sleep.

To My Father

Snow Tree Books
P.O. Box 546
Peabody, MA 01960-7546
www.snowtreebooks.com

Printed in China
ISBN 0-9749006-1-3
Library of Congress Control Number: 2004091506

First Edition